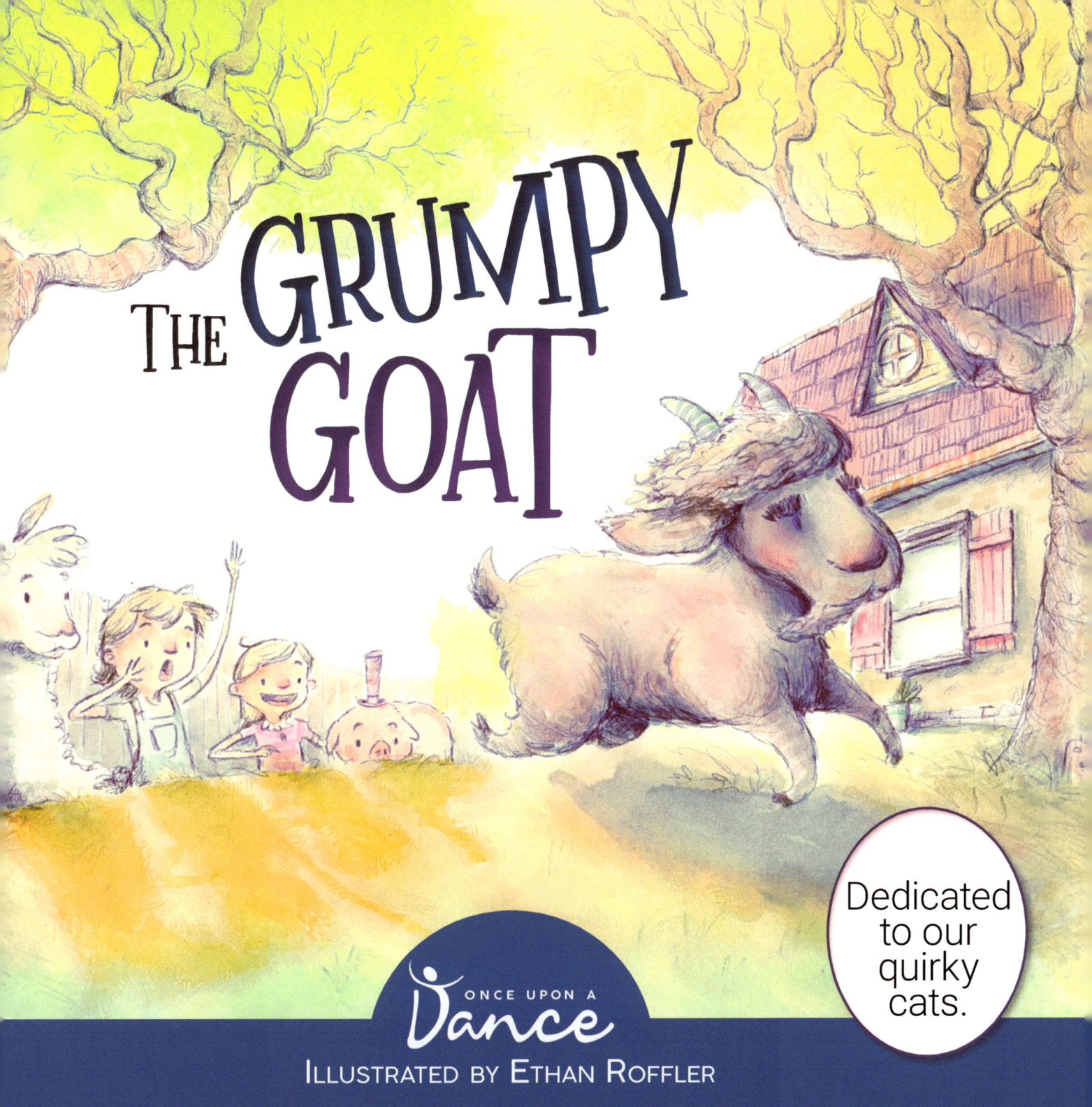

The Grumpy Goat: A Dance-It-Out Creative Movement Story

© 2022 Once Upon a Dance (Redmond, WA)
Illustrated by Ethan Roffler
All royalties donated to Seattle Humane
Photos @ Once Upon a Dance   Interior Fonts: Avenir Next, Dancing Script, Cocogoose, Metropolis

All rights reserved. No part of this publication may be reproduced, distributed, or transmitted in any form or by any means, without the prior written permission of the publisher, except for brief quotations for review/promotional purposes and other noncommercial uses permitted by copyright law. Teachers are welcome to use the story for class; please give Once Upon a Dance credit.

Each Dance-It-Out! story is a performance for the imagination stage with Ballerina Konora as an optional movement guide. In this story, siblings Aspen and Sycamore live with Mee and Mama on Maple Street. Animal chaos ensues when they get a goat to help with blackberry bushes taking over the backyard.

LCCN: 2022907646
ISBN: 978-1-955555-44-9 (paperback); 978-1-955555-43-2 (ebook); 978-1-955555-45-6 (hardcover)

Juvenile Fiction: Animals: Farm Animals
(Juvenile Fiction: Interactive Adventures; Imagination & Play; Performing Arts: Dance)
First Edition

All readers agree to release and hold harmless Once Upon a Dance and all related parties from any claims, causes of action, or liability arising from the contents. Use this book at your own risk.

Other Dance-It-Out! Titles:
Brielle's Birthday Ball: A Dance-It-Out Creative Movement Story for Young Movers
Joey Finds His Jump!: A Dance-It-Out Creative Movement Story for Young Movers
Dayana, Dax, and the Dancing Dragon: A Dance-It-Out Creative Movement Story for Young Movers
Danny, Denny, and the Dancing Dragon: A Dance-It-Out Creative Movement Story for Young Movers (duplicate)
Princess Naomi Helps a Unicorn: A Dance-It-Out Creative Movement Story for Young Movers
The Cat with the Crooked Tail: A Dance-It-Out Creative Movement Story for Young Movers
Mira Monkey's Magic Mirror Adventure: A Dance-It-Out Creative Movement Story for Young Movers
Belluna's Big Adventure in the Sky: A Dance-It-Out Creative Movement Story for Young Movers
Freya, Fynn, and the Fantastic Flute: A Dance-It-Out Creative Movement Story for Young Movers
Sadoni Squirrel: Superhero: A Dance-It-Out Creative Movement Story for Young Movers
Petunia Perks Up: A Dance-It-Out Movement and Meditation Story
Frankie's Wish: A Wander in the Wonder (A Dance-It-Out Creative Movement Story)
Danika's Dancing Day: A Dance-It-Out Creative Movement Story for Young Movers
Andi's Valentine Tree: A Dance-It-Out Creative Movement Story for Young Movers

Other Once Upon a Dance Series:
Dancing Shapes: Ballet and Body Awareness for Young Dancers (6+)
Konora's Shapes: Poses from Dancing Shapes for Creative Movement & Ballet Teachers
Ballet Inspiration and Choreography Concepts for Young Dancers (ages 8+)

Hello Fellow Dancer,

My name is Ballerina Konora. I love stories, adventures, and ballet, and I'm glad you're here with me!

Will you be my dance partner and act out the story along with the Saps family? I've included some suggested moves. Feel free to use these ideas, the illustrations, or create your own moves. Be safe, of course, and do what works for your body in your space. And feel free to settle in and enjoy the pictures the first time through.

Enjoy!

Konora

Once Upon a Dance, Aspen and Sycamore Saps rushed home to hear Mee and Mama's daily news.

Mee owned a successful hat store. The kids loved to hear about the unusual customers' orders. Some of Mee's recent creations had looked like an alligator, an octopus, and a taco.

Mama was a firefighter and often had exciting stories about her job. Sometimes, Mama would bring a rescued pet home while it waited to be reunited with its owners. Aspen hoped beyond hope that one day soon, a sweet dog or cat would visit the Saps' house on Maple Street and never leave.

Let's re-create those silly hat shapes. Crawl while reaching your arms out like an alligator mouth and snap, snap, snap. Lie on the floor and move your arms and legs all around like an octopus. For an extra challenge, try making the octopus balanced on your bottom. Then make the shape of a taco by bringing your feet and hands together in the air.

Mama saved people all the time, but the kids especially loved to hear about animal rescues. Mama always saved her most exciting rescue stories for dinnertime—cats stranded in trees, birds trapped in nets, and even a goat that was stuck on a ledge for days while the firefighters waited for a special ladder to arrive.

Once, Mama pulled some tiny ducklings out of a sewer where they'd gotten stuck. She said their quackful waddle back to mother duck was the cutest thing she'd ever seen.

Let's be like the cat and reach one leg behind like a tail. Then flap your bird wings, and pretend you're a goat standing on a high cliff.

Now, let's get our quack, quack going as we bend our knees, squat down, and take tiny steps forward. Flapping your arms might help you balance.

For Mama, every day was unique. She never knew whether it would be calm or chaos. During quiet times, the firefighters practiced firefighting skills. They attached hoses to fire hydrants, climbed ladders, and crawled under obstacles.

The Saps lived close to the fire station, and whenever sirens blared nearby, Aspen and Sycamore ran to the porch, hoping to see Mama's truck rush past. The firefighters looked like superheroes as they drove down the street.

Drag the heavy hose to a hydrant, then attach the hose and spin the dial to tighten it. Climb a pretend ladder—march while you reach up and pull your arms down. Lie belly-down on the ground and scooch yourself forward with your elbows.

Let's make the siren noises as we zoom to an emergency. Then pretend to be the kids running out to wave at the trucks.

Maple Street got lots of sunshine, and the Saps' grass and flowers thrived. Bunnies from the nearby fields loved to bounce around in the long grass, their little noses twitching as they moved between the flowers.

Wild blackberry bushes also grew in the yard, and once a year, the whole family took the day off to make blackberry jam. But those blackberry bushes grew a little too well, and they reached high up the sides of the house. Poor Sycamore woke up screaming one night. She'd had a nightmare that branches had covered the roof and swallowed their entire home!

Bunny time—hop, hop, hop, and shake your bunny tail. Can you move slowly, like a flower reaching toward the sun?

Next, imagine fingers and limbs extending, and reach your vines higher and higher, like the blackberry bushes.

Aspen checked on the computer for ways to control blackberry bushes, and one of the suggestions was to get a goat. "Wouldn't a backyard goat be fantastic?" Aspen asked.

Sycamore stamped her leg on the ground with an enthusiastic chant: "Goat, goat, goat, goat!"

Mama shook her head so hard the kids thought she might fall over, but then she looked thoughtful and said, "I wonder if that goat we rescued is still at the farm?"

Type on your pretend keyboard with your fingertips and thumbs. Make small, quick bounces like Aspen might while explaining the goat idea. Then switch to Sycamore—lift your knee and stomp your leg down four times while chanting *goat* a little louder with each stomp.

Shake your head like Mama, slowly at first, then with more force and speed. Wait a moment before putting a finger to your lips as you reconsider.

Later that night, while the kids were washing the dishes, Mama and Mee came in with an announcement. "Guess what! We're getting a goat."

"For real?" asked Aspen, and when Mama nodded her head yes, the kids held hands and joyfully spun around.

Mee scooped up some dish soap bubbles, tossed them in the air, and blew them toward the children. "Well, we don't have to if you're not interested," Mee teased. The kids giggled and popped the bubbles with their fingers, toes, and elbows.

Hold hands with a real or imaginary friend and spin around each other, moving your feet in a circular path. Try popping bubbles with your fingers, toes, and elbows. What other body parts could you use to pop bubbles?

The very next day, a truck pulled up in the driveway. A man hopped out, walked to the back, opened the door, and grabbed a rope. At the end of the rope was a sweet but grumpy-looking goat. "This is Gary. Now, where are those pesky blackberry bushes?" he asked.

Aspen pointed to the backyard, and Sycamore skipped ahead.

Steer your pretend truck into the narrow driveway. Go around to the back where you pull open the door, and gently lead the goat out.

Point one finger like Aspen. Then lift your knees high as you march or skip in a half-circle.

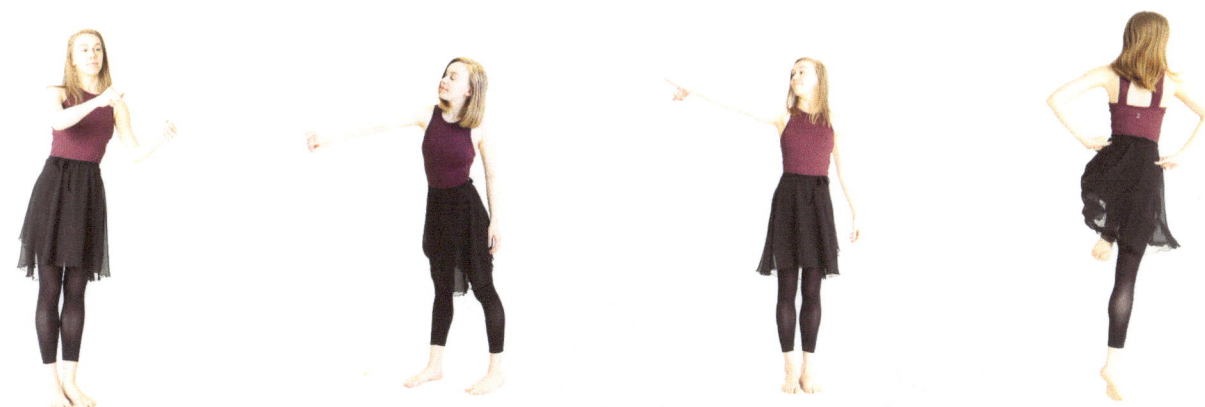

When the kids came home the next day, Gary was sitting in the corner of the yard farthest from the blackberries with his head bent over so far he seemed upside down. He'd only nibbled one dandelion, and he hadn't touched a single blackberry branch!

Mama called the farm for advice.

"We didn't had Gary very long, but maybe he's lonely," the farmer said. "He might enjoy company."

The truck was back in the driveway the very next day. The driver got out, went around to the back, and opened the door.

Tuck your head low like Gary. Use your hand and fingers to make a pretend telephone call. Then, here we go again: drive your truck, hop out, and pull open a door. Any guesses what animal the farmer brought?

This time the rope was attached to a pig. The driver led the pig to the backyard. As if announcing royalty, he circled his hand, gave a bow, and said, "This is Pezi Pot Belly the third, at your service."

The kids laughed. They reached their hands out toward Pezi, and the little pig sniffed and nuzzled their fingers.

Walk sideways as if leading the pig around to the backyard while you keep an eye on the animal. Now, just like the farmer, circle your fingertips as if drawing small circles in the air. Make an extra big circle and bring your hand across your belly. Lean forward in a bow.

Laugh like the kids as you reach out and hold still so the pig can come and say hello.

Wherever Gary went, Pezi was his shadow. But Gary wanted nothing to do with the poor pig. Sometimes, Gary angrily turned around with a "Meh-eh-eh." Pezi would then lounge in the sunshine for a while before trying again, always hoping to be Gary's new best friend.

When the kids came outside, Pezi would take a break from following Gary around to scurry over for back scratches. She lifted her piggie shoulders up and down and made happy little snorting sounds—always three quick sniffs in and two snorts out.

The kids waited and watched. Even though Gary was never nice to her, Pezi didn't give up and always tried to inch just a little closer to the goat, only to be chased away.

Lie on the floor, lift your arms and legs in the air, and roll around like Pezi. Nuzzle and cuddle against a gentle hand and move your shoulders all around for a little back scratch. Can you count three sniffs like you are smelling something, then blow two puffs out through your nose?

Mama called the farm. "Pezi is very sweet, but Gary still doesn't seem happy. And our blackberry bushes keep growing!"

The farmer offered to take both of the animals back, but the Saps family wouldn't hear of it. They'd quickly grown quite fond of the little pig. The kids enjoyed tossing snacks in Pezi's direction and watching her catch each one in mid-air.

Sycamore suggested a backyard picnic to spend time with the animals. Pezi enjoyed herself, of course. But Gary wasn't impressed when the whole family each got down on all fours, ate berries, and made mmmm sounds—trying to entice Gary to take a taste.

Pretend to make a phone call again. Move your head side to side and lift your chin higher as if you are catching snacks like Pezi. Get down on all fours and start munching blackberries while making mmmm sounds.

A few days later, Mama had a surprise. "Check the backyard," she said. The kids darted to the window. Outside, a llama was looking at Pezi, who was intently staring at Gary.

"She was standing in the middle of the highway and wouldn't budge," Mama said. "She's lucky a car didn't run her over. Bob lassoed her cowboy-style, and it took four of us to drag her into a trailer. She can only stay until someone comes to claim her, but I thought Pezi might enjoy the company."

Llama time—bend forward and touch your hands to the floor. Stand firm while people push and pull you. Character-switch-a-roo to Bob the firefighter twirling his rope in the air and throwing it over the llama's head.

The llama was friendly, and the kids named her Lulu. She stood patiently whenever anyone brushed her hair, and she enjoyed treats straight from the kids' hands. Lulu ate a couple blackberries each day but seemed to only enjoy them as a kind of dessert.

Lulu wanted to play with the other animals, but neither Pezi nor Gary wanted to be friends! Gary stayed huddled in one corner of the yard. Pezi kept trying to creep into Gary's space, but if Lulu came near, Pezi chased her away. Then Lulu would stick out her tongue and blow raspberries in protest.

"I really wish that grumpy goat would eat the bushes and all the animals would get along," Aspen said.

Pretend to brush someone's hair, or be like Lulu and have someone brush your hair. Reach your hand out, palm up, like the kids offering Lulu a treat.

Stick out your tongue as you lean forward like an annoyed Lulu. Then keep your lips together and push air out of your mouth to blow a raspberry.

One beautiful sunny Tuesday, Aspen found Gary smack-dab in the middle of the yard with his hoof up, shading his eyes from the sun. Aspen patted him on his nose and scratched his back. Gary nuzzled his head under Aspen's shoulder. Suddenly, he looked up, gave a hard stare, grabbed Aspen's sunglasses in his mouth, and ran away.

Can you balance with two feet and one hand touching the ground? Try lifting one arm above your head in this position—it might take some practice. Pretend to gently touch somebody's nose and scratch their back. Now, try the hard stare—lift your head, open your eyes wide, and only look at one thing while you count to three. Grab those sunglasses by opening your mouth and reaching your lips sideways to snatch them up. For an extra challenge, how fast can you move on your hands and feet?

Aspen chased after Gary. "Hey! Why'd ya steal my glasses, you grumpy goat?" Gary ran back into his favorite corner with the glasses in his mouth. "Why DID you steal my sunglasses?" Aspen repeated, then wondered aloud, "Maybe you're only grumpy because you don't like the sunshine?"

Aspen told Sycamore the news. They brought out a tent, opened it up, and hammered the stakes into the dirt. Gary trotted over and lay down in the tent's shade. He kicked his legs up in the air and tapped them together. The kids stared as Gary stood on his hind legs, hop-twirled around, and then kicked his back feet up in the air.

Let's hammer the stakes ten times. Then switch to Gary—lie on your back with your arms and legs above you. Tap your feet together while you clap your hands. For a super-duper challenge, try alternating your feet and hands—my brain gets pretty confused with that one!

Stand up and bend your knees. See if you can jump four times while you spin around in the air. Put your hands on the floor and lift your feet off the ground for just a second.

Aspen and Sycamore high-fived. Gary wasn't grumpy anymore!

Sycamore pulled a few dandelions for Gary, and he happily chomped on the yellow flowers. The goat's lips moved quickly, and dandelion stems and leaves cascaded to the ground.

Aspen put on gloves, yanked out a blackberry stem, and held it out to Gary, trying to entice him out of the tent. But the goat wouldn't leave the tent's shade. Aspen brought the stem inside the shade and Gary ate it right up! "Well, this isn't as easy as I hoped, but I suppose it's one way to get rid of those bushes."

Aspen smiled, clapped, and said to Sycamore, "Gary gave me an even better idea!"

Give someone a high-five. Reach down to pick the dandelions with your thumb and a finger. Switch-a-roo to noisy Gary crunching and munching—smack your lips and tongue together.

Pull on a pretend glove and wiggle your fingers into place. Put one leg forward and lean on that foot to pull a blackberry stem. Lean back and tug the branch loose. Reach the branch out and make little kissing noises like Aspen might to encourage Gary to eat the berries. Finally, smile and clap.

Do you like Gary's new outfit?
What a silly goat!

Thee End! The end.
(My Grandpa always ended stories
this way, and I like to share the fun.)

Thanks for being my dance partner.

Love,

Konora

Feedback Favor?

Kind feedback makes us less grumpy!

We'd love to know what you think and would be immensely grateful for an honest review (from a grown-up) at Amazon, Goodreads, or on social media: @Once_UponADance.

Once Upon a Dance's twenty-three books are mother-daughter collaborations. We were both immersed in the ballet world until the pandemic, and it took a lot of learning to publish the stories. We check for reviews daily, and hearing our books made someone happy is always appreciated.

Konora's Kitties

Visit www.CreativeMovementStories.com/cats if you'd like to learn about our silly cats, the inspiration for this story.

THE DANCE-IT-OUT! COLLECTION

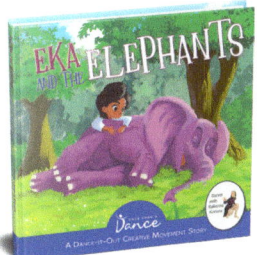
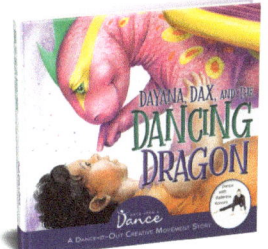
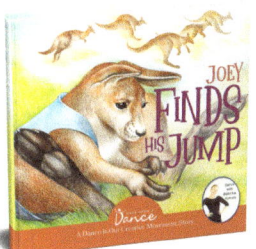
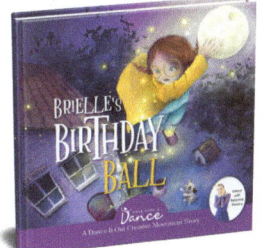
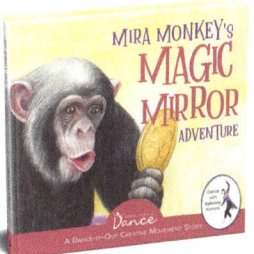
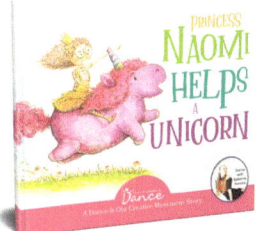
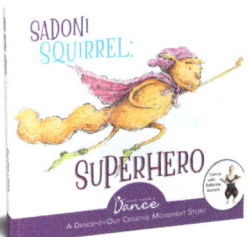
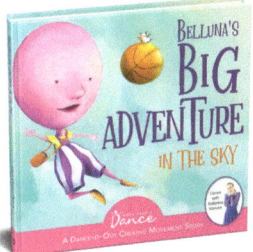
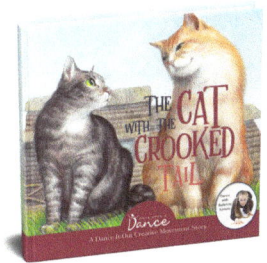

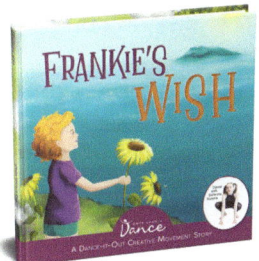
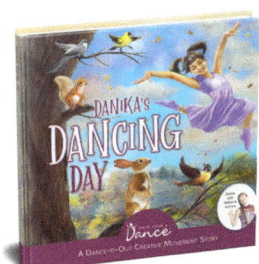

Once Upon a Dance

SERIES CATALOG ALSO INCLUDES:

DANCING SHAPES · KONORA'S SHAPES · BALLET INSPIRATION

www.OnceUponADance.com

Watch for Subscriber Bonus Content

Printed in the USA
CPSIA information can be obtained
at www.ICGtesting.com
LVHW071941011123
762649LV00019B/687